BECKET'S BONES

TO THE

BLITZ

SEVEN MORE CANTERBURY TALES
FOR CHILDREN

by

MARJORIE LYLE

(Author of *Seven Buried Canterbury Tales*)

PUBLISHED by CHOUGH PRESS
25 Rough Common Road, Canterbury, Kent, CT2 9DL

PRINTED by MICKLE PRINT LTD
Westminster Road, Vauxhall Industrial Estate, Canterbury, Kent CT1 1YY

ISBN 0-9529383-1·

D1471930

Dear Reader,

Most people felt Canterbury was finished when Henry VIII shut the monasteries and pulled down St Thomas Becket's famous pilgrim shrine. These stories are about two real and eight imaginary children who lived through those days and other exciting times during the next 400 years. When German bombers flattened so much of Canterbury in 1942 many felt again that the city could never revive. We all know today how wrong they were.

But whatever is going on in the world as we grow up, we care most about what our families and friends expect and think of us. Some people have more to put up with than others but, like these children long ago, we will all have hard choices to handle.

I hope you enjoy these tales, for the school children to whom I read the last set gave me a lot of good advice. I hope too that you will look out for the buildings and museum objects in the stories when you visit this surprising old city.

Marjorie Lyle

For Helen and Ronan

ACKNOWLEDGEMENTS

My thanks go to the following, who retain their copyrights:

PAUL CRAMPTON for the use of the Blitz photographs.

COLIN DUDLEY for his Shrine reconstruction on the front cover.

KENNETH REEDIE and Canterbury Museums for the use of the copyright pictures credited by each reproduction.

PAUL BENNETT and the Canterbury Archaeological Trust Ltd for the central Canterbury reconstruction drawing, and also Longmarket and Central Canterbury on fire, June 1st 1942, seen from the Cathedral (front cover).

CANTERBURY ENVIRONMENT CENTRE for the map of St George's parish.

MARGARET FISHER for access to her research on Canterbury's Walloon and Huguenot community.

CONTENTS

On view in the Canterbury Heritage Museum / Canterbury Museums ©

Nobody knows whether this figure came from a church or monastery, so I could invent its part in my story. Very few statues, even without their heads, survived fifty years of vandalism after Henry VIII's day.

TOM, DICK AND HARRY

'Chuck us over some of those plums you managed to nick from the Refectory,' said Tom, as orphan Dick's sharp, pointed face popped through the hatch after his chip basket.

'Sorry I'm late; there was a huge pile of washing up,' Dick panted as he flopped down beside Tom and Harry, already lolling in the sweet, new hay of the stable loft that September afternoon in Canterbury Priory in 1538.

'Every Tom, Dick and Harry was made for you three!' Tom's mother had said tartly, as he grabbed the fresh roll left as a present for his Dad, the Precincts porter. They had always brought something to eat to their snatched meetings in this favourite hidey-hole. Harry had brought a chunk of honeycomb, for he'd been helping his father with the bees, which kept the monks in sweetening and the wax from which they made the myriad candles burning round the great pilgrim shrine of St Thomas in the Cathedral.

As they had grown up, it seemed as if nothing could ever change in their enclosed world, serving the priory monks. Now, at twelve, they knew that only 59 monks rattled round the huge buildings once housing 150 and that King Harry was changing everything in the world outside. Today's news rubbed it in.

'I'll never forget that herald who lodged with us last year,' said Tom. 'Thirty days running he marched into the Cathedral in his gaudy tabard, blowing his silver trumpet at the four corners of the shrine to call 'Bishop Becket to appear before the King's court in London on charges of treason.' As if a corpse could rise after lying murdered in his tomb these 350 years! Now Dad has heard today that the judge has pronounced him guilty 'in his absence.' His bones are to be burnt and his goods - our famous treasures - are forfeited to the King.'

'If the shrine goes, Dad's and my jobs go too as a start,' Harry said, 'but who can stand up to our King Harry? He hanged two of our monks at Tyburn with Nun Barton for speaking out against his divorce. Then last year he shut down our three friaries and Father Stone is in prison now for daring to say boo to the King's officer. Even St Augustine's Abbey has grovelled to the King and given itself up.'

'You'd not have kept those jobs long anyway, with precious few pilgrims, save the odd foreigner,' Dick chipped in, 'How long can the Priory last if the shrine goes? As it is there are two of us servants for every monk. They think the King daren't touch them, but there's few in Canterbury would stick up for them.'

'True enough,' Tom replied. 'Dad's been to all the closing down sales - he picked up a nice carved chair and a silver spoon cheap. If the Priory goes and he loses his gatekeeper's job, he's planning to snap up a cottage when the monks' properties are sold, so we'll have somewhere to live.'

In the gloomy silence which fell on them came Tom's fierce whisper, 'I'm called after St Thomas and I don't see why his shrine should come down just to deck out the King's women in our saint's jewels.'

'HUSH ! That's treason,' spat out his mates, as if the very stable walls had ears.

'If you plan on saving some relic while there's time, count me in, for I'll need something to sell in France,' whispered Dick. 'I'm an orphan and without the monks' charity I have no future here even as a washer-up.'

Harry broke in with a sigh, 'There's an end to 'Tom, Dick and Harry'!

Tom will be a banned name; Dick will be fled or hanged for thieving and only Harry here has a future. The King's making a palace out of old St Augustine's Abbey. I'll get a job in the garden there, but I'll help you first. I hate to see the King's men with their lists, marking off what can stick to their own sly fingers on its way to the King's treasury.'

'Young varmints ! Get you down.' A furious bellow came from below. Harry had been popping plum stones through a crack in the floor, little knowing their target was the stable man's bald head.

'We must think hard and fast,' said Tom. 'Let's plan everything, same time and place, the day after tomorrow.'

When they next met they had no clearer idea of what they could find or what they could do with it, only a fierce determination that some relic of Canterbury's saint should stay in his city until times changed again.

'The officers have chained a great mastiff by the door and have been ordered to patrol outside all night,' Tom reported.

'Luckily Dad and I are on duty as watchers at the shrine tomorrow night, with old Brother Dunstan who always nods off,' said Harry, 'but I don't know how I can let you in.'

'The Sub-Prior has toothache and can't sleep, so the Infirmarer has given him some poppy-powder for his evening wine. If I can get some, your Dad and Brother Dunstan can have sweet dreams,' Dick grinned. 'I'll bring some scraps for the mastiff; the poor brute looks half-starved.'

'That just leaves the guards, but it's been so wet the last two nights they've been glad enough to come over to the gatehouse,' Tom put in. 'It's become quite a habit since the younger one took a fancy to my sister, red hair and all.'

As they parted Harry reminded them, 'It's our last chance. Tomorrow at 9 o'clock, then, when the monks have gone to bed. I'll be sure the door's unlocked if you two can lure the guards away and feed the dog.'

It was another night of heavy thundery rain and gusty wind. Dick cowered behind a buttress and watched Tom cross from the lighted gateway to invite the two sopping watchmen over to warmth and comfort. Dick crept out to find the poor dog as wet as everything else. He had a good haul of scraps from the monks' dirty dishes and before the last crumb had gone he heard Tom's squelching steps. They eased the door gently open into another world of space and silence, of stairways and shadows and the looming presence of long-dead monks and bishops, whose carved effigies lay below the splendid canopies of their stone tombs. Harry met them by the pilgrim steps, worn hollow by the feet of three centuries, which led up to St Thomas' shrine.

'Father and Brother Dunstan are talking politics. I said it was boring, but I'd bring them a treat,' whispered Harry, 'Give me the wine; I'll join you when it has worked, but wait for a bit,' he added.

Tom and Dick crouched down, gazing at the shrine, raised on its carved arched base. The huge wooden cover which protected the coffin and its treasure at night was winched up, for the next morning the demolition was to begin. In front stood the altar with its white and red velvet cover, embroidered with gold wire and pearls. The coffin itself winked with gold, silver and innumerable jewels.

'There is the great ruby of France which King Louis gave, when his son recovered from the point of death,' breathed Tom.

'Look! The seals on the coffin are broken,' said Dick. 'If you could climb up and get a hand inside you might at least get some cloth wrapping, if no bones.'

7

'If I could climb on your back, I might get my foot on that saint and reach up,' said Tom.

'Dare you ?' whispered Dick. 'I feel dead Prior Henry's cold breath on my neck and the accusing eye of the great Black Prince, buried here so near the saint.'

'We're only trying to save St Thomas from his wicked enemies,' Tom replied.

Dick bent, Tom climbed, the saint's head supported his foot and he inched the coffin lid open to feel inside - nothing!

'I think it's empty,' he hissed down at Dick, whose whisper floated back, 'Of course ! We're not the only ones who hate the King's men. The monks themselves will be desperate to save some relics of the saint. What's the betting they broke the seals ?'

Tom objected. 'They'd never take the lot, for if King Harry hears there's nothing to burn in there, he'll have them all strung up like Nun Barton.'

'Perhaps they're planning to put some other old bones back in there instead before tomorrow,' suggested Dick.

They heard rapid feet pattering and Harry panted up.

'Dad and Brother Dunstan are fast asleep but I can hear voices. Some others are coming, so hide quickly.' Tom began to scramble down but fell in a heap on to Dick. The saint's head had snapped off and the little robed figure, detached from its base, lay beside him. Snatching it up he tiptoed after the others, past the square tomb of King Henry IV and his Queen, to crouch behind the wooden screen of the King's chapel to stare horrified through the lattice.

'Four thousand, nine hundred and ninety nine and three quarters ounces of gold; five thousand, two hundred and eighty six ounces of plain silver; two precious mitres of silver-gilt overworked with pearls and precious stones; nine pontifical rings and a golden shell adorned with divers precious stones.' The voice of the cross-eyed official from London intoned from a long inventory list.

'And who is to say how many is 'divers precious stones' ?' replied the oily voice of his fat friend.

'Jewels will be the easiest to filch, the handiest to hide and the hardest to trace if we go for the small stuff - pearls and the like.' They began to snip away gold wire and seed pearls from the altar frontal when they in their turn stood frozen by the distant sound of chanting.

'The monks are coming to Night Office; we must go,' whispered cross-eyes.

'And so must we,' breathed Harry, 'But where has Dick sloped off to? I hoped if he stayed with us we'd keep him to our task rather than his light-fingered pilfering'.

'Everyone is out for himself tonight,' Tom sighed. 'We shall never know what the monks are up to, for we dare not linger now.' As they crept out, there was Dick beside them again, but it was too dark to see whether he blushed, if he looked guilty or seemed out of breath.

Over the next days, as the carts creaked through the gate past Tom's house, bound for the King's Treasury in the Tower of London; as the shrine of Canterbury's great saint was demolished and piles of bones were burnt, nobody had time nor attention for three boys whose future was now so unsure. Nobody saw them bury the small statue saved from King Henry's men.

Three years later, on a summer afternoon, Tom led a packhorse back from Oaten Hill, laden with hay for the Precincts. He worked now for the Dean and Chapter of the New Foundation. They needed their horses tended quite as much as the monks before them. The Priory of Christchurch and its 59 monks had lasted less than two years after the shrine had gone. For Tom, Harry's forecast had proved all too true. By Royal Proclamation, 'St Thomas' name, images, feasts, collects and commemorations' had been erased throughout the kingdom, so that even a reference in a book was carefully cut or scratched out. As he turned into Newingate he bumped into Harry, carrying a box of plants.

'Hey, let's stop for a drink at the 'Flying Horse' across the road,' he said. 'This box is heavy and I can't plant anything out until the sun is off the bed under the Queen's chambers at the old Abbey Palace. You know, I work in the garden there.'

'What happened to Dick ?' asked Tom when they were settled with their ale. 'I remember he went over there with you when the Abbey church was being pulled down.'

'He went off with one of the loads of stone sent over to France to mend the walls of Calais. He always said his best hope lay abroad', Harry replied.

'I wonder how much he did steal that night,' mused Tom.

'I daresay St Thomas would forgive him if he did take anything. It was always the monks' job to care for poor orphans. If he could no longer have a home at the Priory, even as a washer-up, the saint would want to help him still,' Harry answered. 'What I'd like to know is what happened to Becket's bones? Did the monks manage to hide some ? Where do you think they'd choose ? All sorts of rumours are flying around, but I'll lay my money the King did a thorough job of burning anything at all that would keep St Thomas' name and cult alive.'

'Look over there,' said Tom. 'Perhaps St Thomas has got the last laugh after all.'

They looked at the city's arms waving lazily on the flag atop Newingate. There was the King's lion on it, tongue lolling greedily out, but, on a white ground proudly strutted three black, red-footed birds - Cornish choughs or Beckets, as ordinary folk call them.

You can see a similar headless figure to Tom's in the Heritage Museum.
Rumours about Becket's bones still linger on today.
The 'Flying Horse' is still a pub; it was newly-built then.

TOM MARLOWE AND THE SPANISH ARMADA

'Curse these mosquitoes; my teeth chatter so with fever who knows whether I will live to finish what I start in this year of grace 1626. After all, I'm fifty and glad enough to lay my bones here in Jamestown, Virginia, by my poor wife and child. The hunger took them in those bad early days of the colony. Nowadays, my mind keeps going back to Armada year, 1588, in far-off Canterbury, for I reckon that saving my brother Christopher was my best deed. Perhaps my sisters have children in Canterbury, but the Marlowe name will die with me unless it lives on in Christopher's plays.

When I was born in April 1576, my brother Kit, as we called him, was twelve and the eldest, with four quarrelsome sisters between him and me. Like our Dad, John Marlowe the cobbler, he was a firebrand even then and full of new enthusiasms which he'd dash off into verses. My earliest memory is sitting on his shoulders among the crowds and garlands in the High Street to catch sight of England's hero, Sir Philip Sidney. He had come to meet John Casimir, the Polish warrior who had held the Turks at bay. While the retinue of gentlemen in brilliant liveries and their splendid horses passed by in his wake, Kit turned shining eyes on me,

'Oh Tom, there's a man who can dazzle the Queen at court one day and serve her against the Catholic Spaniards the next and write the most wonderful verses too. One day I'll leave this dreary little town behind me to make such a name for myself in London.'

All England was to mourn when Sir Philip died in battle against the Spanish in the Netherlands, giving his last drink to a wounded comrade. By then, Kit had long ago left us behind to study in Cambridge. He had only once come home on some mysterious errand to France of which he would tell us nothing.

July 12th 1588 turned into a terrible day for me. I was a choirboy at the Cathedral and had to be at practice at 8 of the clock but I woke late. Stumbling into the street, a pail of slops from our neighbour's upstairs window landed, splat, all over me. I had no time to change and panted into the practice room stinking like a sewer.

'Sing me a G-sharp, quickly, boy ! If you think that because your tearaway brother is storming the London groundlings at the 'Rose' theatre

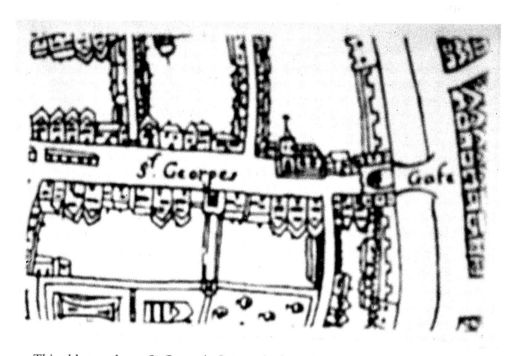

This old map shows St George's Gate and where Tom and Kit met in the story.
It was earlier called Newingate and was where Tom bumped into Harry
at the end of the last story
Their home, bombed in 1942, was on the corner of the lane
below the word 'George's'.

This is Christopher Marlowe's only known signature,
made when he witnessed a will on a rare visit to Canterbury.

with his *Tamburlaine* you can come late and smelly to practice, think again.' The choirmaster reached out with his baton and struck me sharply on the head. Once practice was over and we tumbled downstairs to the Precincts, Will Corkine, the lute-player's son, leapt on my back, 'We always knew you were mad like Kit. They say he's an atheist and curses God; they say he's an alchemist - but fools' gold is all he'll ever find and even if he's a playwright they say he's a spy, spy, spy.'

'You're just jealous' I screamed, clouting Will in the stomach. We rolled on the ground, our mates in a ring egging us on.

A cold foreign voice interrupted us. 'Are you young gentlemen practising to fight the Spanish troops when they land from the great Armada? I hope for England's sake that your militia is more skilful than you.' A thin, bearded face, a beaky nose and smart black doublet and hose bent over me.

'Do I understand, boy that you are brother to Christopher Marlowe whose play *Tamburlaine* is the talk of London?

I picked myself up as the others melted away and the stranger walked me round to the monks' ruined cloisters nearby.

'Your brother's path crossed mine once in Rheims, back in `85 when we were on opposing business. He was lucky then not to end up in the gutter with his throat slit as his friend did. Do you expect him home now?'

'No, sir, Kit has only come back once since he left for Cambridge eight years ago. It grieves my parents sorely.'

'He dabbles in dangerous matters, ill-suited to a young poet and would do well to leave high matters of war and statecraft to grown men - tell him so when you see him. I am not the only one who studies his movements and dogs his footsteps.' Turning on his heel he vanished into the Cathedral as if he had been a ghost.

Service was long that evening with a special anthem for the danger from Spain, 'Oh Lord, arise and let thine enemies be scattered.' I made my way home pondering who the stranger was. Will had said that Kit was a spy; was that why he had come home before and why he had gone off to Rheims ?

I came home to another blazing row. My Father was booting the tailor John Jordan through the door while sister Margaret clung screaming to his arm. 'Am I never to wed ? I'm 23 and scorned in the street as an old maid. I'll have none but my John.' I clapped my hands to my ears and took refuge in the lean-to beyond the kitchen where I slept.

It must have been midnight when I was woken by a soft scratching on the shutter. When I opened up a dark figure said, 'Hush ! Let me in Tom, for nobody must know I am here. I need your help badly.'

After so long, how everything that day had brought Kit to mind and here he was, sitting on my bed, his reddish hair catching glints from the tallow candle I lit.

'Why do you leave London when your play goes so well ?' I asked.

'It is one thing to write a play, but after the great Edward Alleyn who plays Tamburlaine is paid and our boss Henslowe pleads all his expenses, I'm the last to get my fee. I'm writing more plays, one about a pact with the Devil and one about a Jew, but I'm dead short of money. I expect you've guessed I sometimes work for the Queen's secret agents abroad. How else would the Privy Council make Cambridge grant me my M.A. degree last year?'

'Now we are at war with Spain what can you do ?' I asked.

'All the more reason, for if the great Spanish fleet can reach Holland and pick up their troops there, who could stop them landing here and how long could the likes of Father and the local militia save Queen Bess? Sir Philip Sidney was ready to die for her sake and where he led I follow, to find out where and in what numbers the Spanish army is gathering.'

I told Kit then of my strange meeting that day.

'Not him ! Not the Spanish priest again,' breathed Kit. 'They must be on to me. I need a horse quick, if our cousin Arthur in Dover is to take me over in his boat tomorrow night.'

'The only nag I know is John Jordan's. He's courting Meg and needs friends in this family. Leave it to me, but I'll have to come pillion with you to ride him back,' I said after a long pause.

'I'll lie up here today then under the bed, if you can get me a bite to eat and I'll meet you outside St George's Gate just before curfew,' Kit replied eagerly.

Early next morning I fetched some bread from the top of the pig bucket and two apples for Kit, then found poor John already opening up his tailor's shop with a doleful face.

'Take cheer,' I said, 'My parents only delay because sister Jane wed too young and died in childbed - I'll do what I can for you, but first I need to borrow your horse for an urgent errand tonight. I promise to have him back by dawn.'

'Bless you, Tom; I'd wait forever for Meg but she grows more desperate by the day,' and John led me to his backyard, where the old grey leant against a wall, a wisp of hay dangling from his mouth.

As I gentled him I thought - what if Kit dies in Holland as Sir Philip did? Could Kit become as great a writer if he got the chance ? How can I stop this fool errand when the other side are already on his scent ? The grey horse stamped crossly as his hay was done and he gave me my idea. So it was that when I met Kit at dusk, by the great east gate to Canterbury, I had a stone and a long, sharp thorn in my pouch. We set off, with me riding pillion behind, until we were well clear of the outskirts and on the Dover Road.

Stop,' I said 'I'm going to be sick any minute.' I slithered off to double over the wayside ditch to retch convincingly. Still bent and groaning, I came back to mount behind again and managed to slip stone and thorn into the grey nag's rear hoof. Clop - clop - clop, on we went steadily with never a sign of trouble and I feared both must have shaken free. Just as we started downhill towards the village of Bridge, a scream and a neigh broke the night air, the horse bucked violently and I was thrown to land with my foot bent awkwardly under me and my forehead cracked open on a tree stump. Jumping down Kit cried, 'How badly are you hurt? Can you walk?' Blood poured down my face, but it was only a gash. However when I tried to rise it was plain I had a broken ankle. 'I'll have to get you home now, no help for it,' muttered Kit ruefully. 'This was the cause of the trouble' and he held up the long thorn. I was glad my blush was hidden by the blood, as I realised that though the thorn had stuck, the pebble must have worked loose.

We had to hammer on St George's gate on our return, for curfew was long past. The gatekeeper, old Mrs Sweeting the vicar's widow, beamed with joy as she opened up, for Kit and her son Len had been mates at the King's School. She fussed over us, bound my ankle and mothered us until dawn.

'I'll have to dream up some new tale about this and say I was coming on purpose to see you all, when I found you injured,' Kit whispered.

'Then put in a word for poor Meg and John Jordan, whose horse this is,' I replied as we rode down the High Street.

'Is it not passing brave to be a king

And ride in triumph through Persepolis !'

There's a quote for you from my *Tamburlaine*. Do you remember Sir Philip's procession in the street here all those years ago ?' Kit called back over his shoulder.

What a welcome awaited us and how my my mother wept and laughed and questioned! Even Father beamed, for Christopher was their first surviving son, the apple of their eye who could do no wrong. He made sure that Margaret and John were betrothed before he took to the road again, but it was to London he headed, not to Dover. For news that the Armada was sighted broke the next day and all England hung on the tales of running naval battles up the Channel and rejoiced when God sent the great wind which scattered what was left of the Spanish fleet. We had another special anthem to practice in choir, 'Now thanks be to God, who giveth us the victory.'

In the great rejoicing the theatres were packed and Kit was kept over-busy writing another four plays in the next four years. During that time I often wondered if I had done right, until that black day in June 1593 when the terrible news came to Canterbury that our Christopher Marlowe was dead, killed in a tavern brawl at Deptford, and buried up there in an unmarked grave.

Although the neighbours put on long faces for my parents' sake, I heard all too much of their gossip at street corners - 'I'm not surprised he came to a bad end!'; 'He always was a tearaway'; 'All the Marlowes are a quarrelsome lot'; 'Look how he set on old Will Corkine, the lute-player, in Mercery Lane last year!' My parents never really got over Kit's death and died within months of each other in 1605. By then I was working in Deptford Royal Dockyard, trying in my spare time to learn the truth of Kit's end, but I only found dead ends and hearsay or a suspicious silence at every turn. At last, I took ship for Virginia in the 'Jonathan' and as I left England for ever I knew at last that I had done right. All my brother's plays and poems were printed, reprinted and performed again and again. Little Canterbury had bred England's first great dramatist. As the white cliffs sank below the horizon, I remembered Kit's words in *Dr Faustus*,

'Cut is the branch that might have grown full straight
And burnèd is Apollo's laurel bough
That sometime grew within this learnèd man.'

The facts we know:

- *Thomas Marlowe, baptised 15th April 1576, recorded as Cathedral Chorister 1589.*

- *A Thomas Marlowe, 'governor's man', who had arrived in the 'Jonathan', recorded near Jamestown, Virginia, in 1624.*

- *Margaret Marlowe (1565 - 1636) married John Jordan, tailor, in 1590.*

- *Christopher Marlowe, born 1564, killed in suspicious circumstances at Deptford, aged nearly 29. King's School, Canterbury, and Corpus Christi College, Cambridge. M.A. 1587 at request of Privy Council.*

- Tamburlaine *produced 1588 by Henslowe's Admiral's Men with Edward Alleyn in title role. Also* Dr Faustus, The Jew of Malta, Edward II *and* The Massacre at Paris.

- *John and Katharine Marlowe died in 1605. Thomas, unlike their daughters, does not appear in their wills.*

JOE'S CHRISTMAS

'It's not my fault my mother saw the white witch's one-eyed cat when she carried me.

It's not my fault I was born club-footed and hump-backed; I say she took fright when Father fell down the wine-cellar steps the day I was born.

It's not my fault my elder sister, Anne, was born as beautiful as the day, or that the twins are both girls too.'

These were the thoughts running through my head as I rubbed my leg, shaking with weariness, that January evening and wondering how we could manage now Father and Anne's suitor Robert were both in jail and in danger of hanging. Although Mother always said 'If you don't like it, you must learn to lump it,' Father would rub in daily, in a hundred different ways, how he needed a strong son to help him run the Sun Inn by the Cathedral gate. I couldn't heave casks or run up and down steep steps or even fetch and serve without scornful or pitying looks.

Our troubles really started last Christmas Eve of 1647, but all my childhood years had been studded with disasters. Of course, we are all staunch Anglicans or how else would Father lease Canterbury's best inn from the Dean and Chapter, so our dreadful civil war hit us hard.

I remember when I was seven in '42, the soldiers smashing my hump against the gate as they charged into the Cathedral looking for arms and how I snivelled at Mother's knee as they rolled back demanding drink and lighting their tobacco pipes with torn up service books. I remember the almighty smash on our doorstep when Blue Dick Culmer 's puritans pulled Christ from his niche above the gate, as if he'd not done enough that day, beheading the saints and angels and boasting of 'rattling down proud Becket's glassy bones' from the Cathedral's stained glass windows. I remember Mr Somner, the Cathedral Registrar, getting us to hide part of the lovely font behind Mother's pot-herbs in the yard until times were better. Then, a year later, I remember Mother's tears as she tried on my first black suit. I thought as usual she was crying about my hump, but she told me how they'd beheaded our Archbishop Laud on Tower Hill in London.

But to get back to Christmas Eve, when the puritans ruling the roost in Maidstone forbade us to hold any service, sermon or celebration on

Christmas Day, but to hold a market instead. The twins had been scolded up to bed, wailing that it wasn't fair and why could they have no Christmas pies, presents and sweetmeats just for a lot of crop-haired puritans. Mother flopped down on a stool and banged the table saying, 'Let's all vow we'll do something tomorrow for God and King. You and I, Anne, can at least stop neighbour Bolton opening her baker's stall, even if we have to buy everything ourselves.'

Anne answered, 'Robert and his gang plan to overturn the market stalls, whatever the Mayor says.'

There was no way I could heave stalls over but I saw something I could do. 'I'll take Mother's meat cleaver and help to guard the Cathedral door while the sermon's preached; we'll not let the Mayor's men stop our service.' It was a shame I had to catch the pitying look flashing from Father's eye to Mother's.

So there I stood among the folk of all ages, armed anyhow, on Christmas morning, eyeing the twelve miserable stall-holders who had turned out, when Robert's lot rushed through the gate and started up-ending trestles and spilling the goods. The Mayor and Sheriff, cudgels in hand, were close on their tails and as a stick cracked down on him, Robert whirled round and felled the Mayor in the mud, tearing his cloak. From the ground he roared to the constables to put Robert and his mates in jail but they broke loose, hooting and jeering, and began lobbing two footballs about. One came my way, but when I tried to throw it back Robert called out,

'Keep out of it! This is too hot for you, little one-leg,' and off they tore towards the High Street, where the match surged up and down all day, driving the Aldermen and Councillors indoors.

When I reached the 'Sun,' Father was up on a chair hanging up a holly-bush and calling out, 'Nothing to pay and welcome, gentlemen, for God, King Charles, and Kent.'

Just then the crumpled figure of Culmer, the puritan minister, came tearing towards us, chased by a mob from the 'Saracen's Head' and all my past and present hurts came bubbling up. There, where he had dared to pull down Our Saviour Christ, I pelted him with mud-balls. 'Here's one ball-game I can play,' I muttered vengefully to myself.

By the Monday things were hotter still. Villagers from round about came in to join in the fun, cracking the Sheriff's skull and the Mayor's windows and locking up the puritans. Then some of the King's men arrived saying that King Charles had escaped from Parliament's prison on the Isle of Wight. These cavaliers lodged with us while they seized the city's weapon store and handed out arms to a thousand men. You guessed it; Robert and his friends were the first volunteers and went off to guard Canterbury's gates from the Trained Band army sent from Maidstone to besiege us.

Some of our Councillors soon saw it was all up and persuaded us to lay down our arms, but little good that did. The councillors were packed off to prison in Leeds Castle, the city gates were broken up and burnt and part of the city wall was torn down. For us it was worse still; Robert was imprisoned for his part in the rising and Father for giving aid to the Cavaliers.

So here my thoughts had come round full circle, when Anne came up behind me and gave me a hug.

'It's up to us to help Mother and prove to Dad and Robert that a 'feeble girl' and a 'poor cripple' can run the best inn in town if we divide up the jobs between us.'

I answered her. 'Poor John Bolton next door has his mother to support, now his Dad's in prison too. I'll ask him to do the heavy cellar work and then we'll manage all right.'

'His sister, little plain Jane, is old enough to wash up,' Anne added.

'Just because you're pretty you needn't be so hoity-toity about her - she's not so very plain, either,' I retorted.

Mother had her doubts, but she had the twins and the household to mind, so we found ourselves doing better than we had expected. Business was brisk with so many gentlemen in town and so much anger and plotting about.

The Kentish puritans asked Parliament to have our folk tried by a military court, but up in London it was decided that they should go before the ordinary Assizes here on May 10th. Now Father, as a citizen of Canterbury, would be tried in the City Court at the Guildhall, but Robert lived in Sturry, so he would have to go to the County trial, held at the Castle. Extra soldiers were moved in to guard the two courts and every spare room in town was double-booked. We bullied John Bolton into putting up as a juryman to vote 'not guilty', when we heard they were trying to pack the juries to vote the puritan way.

On the morning of the trials we shut the inn. Mother had gone early to the Guildhall, for Judge Wilde was so blood-thirsty he was calling for hanging under some ancient law or other and she feared for Father's life. Anne had run off to Robert's trial at the Castle where they said Judge Cresheld was more honest. Such a shout of 'God save the King' went up from the crowd there that the start was delayed while they sent for extra Roundhead cavalry. So it was plain the Guildhall trial would start first and that was the place for me. I still arrived late and to begin with I could neither get in nor see.

'Poor little toad! Have you got someone on trial?' One of the guards was looking down at me. 'Hop up there on those fire-buckets; I'll give you a hand, for I'd as soon not be here myself,' he said.

So it was that I was right by the door when the jury came back for the first time. 'What is your verdict?'

'Ignoramus; we don't know and we can't say,' said the foreman.

The judge was furious and called back the witnesses to be re-examined. Then he laid it down, hard and plain, to the jury that they were to find a 'better verdict' of guilty. Out they went; the minutes ticked past; back they filed.

'What is your verdict now ?'

'Ignoramus: we cannot tell,' came the old reply.

Judge Wilde banged on the table, quoting old laws at them, but the lawyers now got up and refused to go on with the cases.

'If we had a jury from hell, they would not give you your verdict,' they answered the judge and the whole Guildhall crowd stamped in approval. As the cheers went up I scrambled down from my perch. If only the Castle lot can learn what the city has decided, maybe it will sway things there too, I thought. Nobody took any notice of a cripple boy as the legal argy-bargy went on, so off I hobbled at my best speed, across the High Street and along Stour Street to the Castle yard.

As I drew near I heard a rhythmic stamping and a chant of 'A King, a King,' from inside, mixed with the jingle of harness, for the troop of roundhead horsemen had arrived to overawe the jurors.

Once again, I found being a cripple as good as a magic cloak and was able to dodge past the soldiers, avoiding the horses' hooves. Good ! There was Anne's golden hair ahead of me. I pulled at her sleeve.

'Dad's all right; they've found a verdict of 'Ignoramus' at the Guildhall

- can you let the jury here know somehow ?' I whispered.

'However did you get through ?' she breathed.

'Being a cripple is handy sometimes,' I grinned.

'Then being a pretty girl may be handy too,' she grinned back, and sidled off. Sure enough all the men were only too happy to make way for her until she reached the line of troops guarding the jury box. Now what? I wondered.

My jaw dropped and I nearly lunged forward as the nearest soldier took out his knife. I needn't have worried; all he did was to cut off a golden curl and let her pass. I watched the concealed grin ripple from face to face along the jury bench as Anne's message was passed but they filed out in all solemnity. In a suspiciously short time they returned.

'How do you find, guilty or not guilty ?' they were asked.

'Ignoramus; we do not know; we cannot convict.'

A great shout of laughter burst out, troops or no troops, as the prisoners were let free.

What an evening that was at the 'Sun.' Anne and I were the heroes of the hour; all our friends had crushed in to greet Father and Robert; Mother couldn't stop laughing and the twins ran everywhere unheeded. But the bar was also filled with rumours that the jurors themselves would be tried, imprisoned, even hanged for their verdicts. A new storm was brewing.

So began that short, sharp time from the end of May to mid-June of 1648 when the men of Kent rose up again for God, King Charles and the old ways of governing. Of course, we were beaten by General Fairfax and, of course, we didn't know then we would have to wait another twelve years to see King Charles II come into his own again.

So here I am on May 25th 1660, outside the city gate on the Dover Road, awaiting our sovereign. The Mayor and Corporation are here in their robes, the church bells are ringing and the streets are decked with green be-ribboned garlands, hung with silver. If I could only remember where that cavalier at our inn told me he'd hidden his silver before he fled in '48 I'd give the lot to His Majesty, along with the City's gift. However, there is Mr Somner with his great book on Canterbury's Antiquities, new-bound in Canterbury leather, to present to King Charles and I've heard that the first baby to be baptised in the restored font is to be Mr Somner's new daughter.

On view in the Canterbury Heritage Museum/Canterbury Museums ©

*Hoards of coins like these turn up by chance where Cavaliers hid them when
they had to flee abroad in 1648 after the Roundheads won.
When England became a Republic, Parliament ordered new coins
without the King's head.*

*In 1994 a new statue of Christ by Klaus Ringwald was put back
in the empty niche above Christchurch Gate in the Buttermarket,
where the 'Sun' Inn is now 'Pizzaland'.*

And here am I, twenty five years of age and in good health. My father and I run the 'Sun' Inn together and I'm wearing a fine new velvet suit made by my brother-in-law, Robert Taylor. He and Anne and their two sons live near us in Burgate. It will be a merry England again and the sun is shining this morning in May. When a man is valued for himself, he doesn't need to remember his lumpy shoulders and feet - and I think I can see Jane Bolton coming up the road to join me. She's just in time to greet the King - God save him!

The Civil war was such a terrible and exciting time that many people, including William Somner, described the true events in this story.
The font is still in the Cathedral.

SUZANNE'S ESCAPE

'Clack - clack - Oh, so obedient
Clack - clack - Oh, so respectable
Clack - clack - Oh, so BORING'

The clatter of our small loom kept pace with my thoughts in the stuffy weaving-loft that sunny Autumn afternoon in 1685. My life was about to change that day, although I did not know it.

My father, Jacques Legros, had gone to a special meeting in the Cathedral crypt, where we had our French church, to see how we could help the new flood of Huguenot refugees from France. King Louis had harried his Protestant subjects more and more lately until they couldn't even worship freely.

We, in Canterbury's French-speaking community, knew all about persecution from our cradles. My great-grandparents had come here in Queen Bess' time to escape the Spanish Catholics in the Netherlands. Grandmother's family had escaped from Calais in an open boat and Grandfather had led the protest when Archbishop Laud tried to make us join English parish churches. Every time I wanted to talk to Anne, the English girl across the road, or grumbled about having to be betrothed to Pierre Boudin, our neighbour's son, or longed to wear the latest bright-coloured fashions, Mother would start again on the old stories,

'Only Canterbury welcomed us in and gave us our own church; only Canterbury let us earn an honest living by our weaving - but there's a price to pay, my girl,' she scolded. 'We keep to ourselves, we sort out our own troubles and we live quietly and so will you !'

One Sunday I refused to cover my curls with a cap for church. She beat me soundly and between each blow spelled it out to me.

'You will marry who we say and when we say (thump). You will go to church twice on Sunday, modestly dressed (thump). You will keep away from the English and work hard (thump).'

She and Father were first cousins and Pierre was my aunt's stepson, but, oh, he was so dreadfully dull ! All he could talk about was weaving and even so, I was twice as quick as him at the new fancy silk weaves.

I had been set to make pattern samples that afternoon and I cheered

The St George's area was badly bombed in 1942, destroying the Marlowe family's cobbler's shop. Only the church tower survives.

IN STORY 3

Joe's father leased the Sun Inn in the Buttermarket. It is now Pizzaland with a new frontage.

IN STORY 1

Tom saw that Henry VIII forgot that Becket's choughs still strutted on the City arms of 1302.

IN STORY 4

Suzanne and her family lived in Turnagain Lane, where you can still see the weaving loft windows.

In Story 7

10 Broad Street is now a lawyer's office.
Here Henrietta came to live with her Gran.

In Story 6

Most of the houses in the stories have found new uses today, but St George's Clock tower alone remains to show where the Marlowes' parish church once stood.

Louise's rich family lived in what is now a hotel facing down St Dunstan's Street.

Story 5

Sidney Cooper and his family really lived here in St Peter's Street. It is now the Chaucer Heritage shop. Many of his paintings hang in the Beaney Institute

On view in the Canterbury Heritage Museum/Canterbury Museums ©

*In time, more of the silk-weavers followed Suzanne to London
where the rich customers lived. Many of the ones left behind married into English
families and took up new trades. You can still find names like
Terry, Lepine and Ridout in the telephone book
and a French service is still held in the Cathedral crypt every Sunday*

myself reciting the lovely names of the gorgeous cloths I would never be allowed to wear - Watered tabby, Estamine, Brocade-damask and Paduasoy, silk cloth from Padua in far-off Italy. We, the Canterbury silk weavers, could copy any cloth the new fashions demanded. The golden sunlight caught the sheen on my sample. On impulse, I defiantly drew a long and shining strand from my golden plait and wove it into my silk sample.

'There ! When that catches some rich lady's eye she will make a fine kerchief of it and perhaps it will go with her one day to a London theatre. How I'd love to do that,' I sighed. I heard the thud of the street door and Father's voice coming up the attic stairs.

'They're expecting up to 1500 refugees this year - almost one for each of us - so I've said we'll take in a family of four. The parents can have Bertrand's room, now he's gone to university in Holland; the grandmother must go in with Suzanne but Paul, the lad, will have to shake down in the weaving loft. They got away from La Rochelle with nothing but their Bible and had a terribly rough voyage.'

'Poor souls, just like Mother's family long ago. For all that, I hope they'll not stop long, for I've promised the Boudins that Pierre can visit over Christmas. I keep hoping Suzanne will warm to him a little, though I sometimes despair of bending her stiff neck to the yoke. When do they arrive ?'

'This evening, wife. I told them it would only be Friday salt cod and cabbage.' Father called up the stairs then, 'Suzanne, pack up now but clear a space for a mattress under the window before you come down.'

As I cleared the floor I found a snippet of blue silk and quickly tied it as a ribbon round the high neck of my dark gown. I pinched my cheeks and teased out a few curls on my forehead. In the kitchen I peeked into the polished bottom of Mother's copper frying-pan and saw a white cap, gold curls, blue eyes, pink cheeks, and the blue ribbon. In a sudden rush of excitement I thought, 'At last, change is coming to Turnagain Lane.'

They came as we scurried round laying the table. Monsieur and Madame Hamel looked really exhausted, but the grandmother was a fierce old lady with sharp and beady black eyes and an acid tongue. Neither Paul nor I of course were expected to speak, but I caught his twinkling eyes resting on me and I was taken by this tall, thin presence with the pale face and the wing of black hair. After supper Madame took her mother up to her bed in my room and Monsieur led Paul towards the loft. On the landing he smiled at me and said, 'Won't you show us the way, Suzanne?'

When we reached the top Monsieur Hamel stopped to look at my samples.

'These are beautiful and so intricate and finely woven. I had no idea the Canterbury weavers were so up to date.'

'Oh, they're only new designs I tried out today,' I replied, 'We'd like to do more but the local people stick to the old fashions and we get our bread and butter from black bombazine for mourning-clothes. I wish I could ever get to London where the grand ladies would buy our fine weaves.' Paul spoke up then,

'We are going to Spitalfields, on the east side of London where our cousins live as soon as we can. I am to finish my apprenticeship with my great-uncle who is a brocade designer.' Just then a cross voice wafted up to us.

'Is that wench never coming to bed ? I need my sleep. If she dallies any longer it will be a shocking waste of a good candle.'

'Goodnight,' called Paul as I scuttled down to Grandmother Hamel, but I had sweet dreams in spite of her snores.

As I yawned my way through the long Sunday service, thinking longingly of the shining autumn day outside, Pierre Boudin took us all by surprise. He asked my parents if he could take our visitor and me for a walk along the river to Fordwich instead of afternoon church. This was unheard of, but Mother smiled on anything to soften me towards Pierre and nudged Father into consenting. We had not gone more than a mile along the towpath when some of Pierre's friends hailed us from the bank where they were fishing.

'These are worth skipping service for, don't you think ?' they shouted, holding up three fat trout. 'But now we've raised a thirst. We know of a snug little alehouse in Sturry and it's time you joined us, Pierre. You've never yet been on a drinking bout.'

'I daren't and anyway I'm in charge of Suzanne and our French visitor,' Pierre stammered back at them.

'Scare-baby ! Can't hold his drink - better run home to mother then before we duck you in the river.' They grabbed Pierre by the collar and breeches to sling him in the water, when Paul broke in, 'I'll gladly escort the young lady home if you plan to join your friends. It will be my great pleasure,' and he bowed gravely towards me. Pierre was dumbstruck. He was far too feeble to stand up to his friends and knew that he must one day prove he was one of the lads, but he certainly had no wish to surrender me to Paul. While he dithered his mates linked arms and frog-marched him off with them.

I shall never forget that golden afternoon, with the river sparkling beside us, while Paul told me the story of his escape from France and of his hopes for a new life in London. When he added, 'Father says you're wasted here. He's never seen such fine work as the piece on the loom,' I told him about how I had woven in some of my hair. Paul stood still and stared hard at me, 'That's one piece that will surely come to London with me as a mascot, then,' he said.

When we reached home my parents were still at church. We knew we should cover up for Pierre until he got back, so we crept upstairs to the weaving loft as quietly as we could, save for the step which always cracked like a bullet by my bedroom door. We waited and waited until supper time but still there was no sign of Pierre. So we slipped down separately and were thankful that young folk never spoke at table until spoken to. Paul had only one polite question to answer about our walk.

Next morning was a different tale altogether. I was in the yard hanging out washing when a terrible row broke out next door. My aunt was weeping and scolding Pierre.

'You've shamed me and your father too, nay the whole street - brought home sick and drunk at dawn, locked out of the city all night, your best clothes ruined. How will we face the Legros family when your case comes up before the Elders.'

I rushed indoors.

'Mother, come quickly ! Hark what's going on.' Mother ran out, dough on her hands, while the accusing voice wailed on.

'It would serve you right if that flighty Suzanne finally turned you down! Yet we are all counting on her dowry and her weaving skills to get us clear of trouble, with Father's business headed downhill and our money draining away.'

'I was only out with the boys. You never let me drink at home so how was I to know how much I could hold ?' Pierre whined.

'Oh! It's my fault I suppose that you were drunk as a pig and we are to be ruined. And who brought Suzanne home, then ?'

'Mother, I can smell your bread burning,' I broke in, for this was coming too close for comfort. As she ran indoors Mother shot me a very sharp look but said no more then.

A heavy thunderstorm hung over our midday meal until Mother and Father retired with long faces to the parlour. The storm finally broke at suppertime when Grandmother Hamel, who had been thoughtfully rolling a little pellet of bread, suddenly spoke in her most icy tones,

'In France we never permit young people of opposite sexes, who are unrelated, to be left alone together. In England you do things differently I see,'

'What do you mean?' said Father. 'What has Suzanne been doing?'

'Yesterday, I took my nap while you were at church, but I was awoken by a loud crack on the stairs. Naturally I feared that it was an intruder, so I took it upon me to investigate the noises coming from the weaving loft.' Grandmother paused dramatically and swept the company with an accusing look but nobody broke the silence. Looking sourly at Paul and me she continued weightily, 'Having satisfied myself that my grandson and your daughter were secretly closeted there together, I later observed their deceitful and separate descent to supper. I now feel it is my Christian duty to bring this matter to light.'

'Is this true, Paul ?' said Monsieur Hamel severely. With a despairing look at me Paul stood stiffly erect, knuckles whitened as he gripped the tablecloth and told it, just as it had happened, all the events of Sunday afternoon.

'You see, we couldn't betray Pierre,' he ended.

'Do not speak of that drunken sot and that scheming underhand lot next door,' my mother broke in. She told of what we heard in the morning and how she and Father had gone to break the betrothal that afternoon. I could hardly breathe for the surge of joy in my stomach and kept my eyes down lest I should laugh out loud - but better still was to come.

Clearing his throat, Monsieur Hamel began to speak quietly. The only sound in the room was a coal dropping in the grate.

'Far be it from we, whom you have so generously sheltered, to bring any disgrace upon a respectable household. Nobody need know of any youthful indiscretion, were you to agree to a new betrothal between Paul here and your Suzanne. From the first I have been astonished at her skill in brocade weaving, which will accord so well with the design business we plan to develop in London. You know how frail is my poor wife's health and your charming daughter would be of the greatest help to her, especially since Grandmère here does not get any younger.'

'It is plain we have a lot to think over and discuss,' said Father,'but this proposal seems a happy solution to our difficulty, if our young folk themselves are agreeable - though they are full young to know their own minds.'

As if on one swivel, every eye turned on Paul and me to stare at our linked hands, for during all this my own hand had crept across the table to grasp Paul's white knuckles still clutching the tablecloth. Suddenly everybody smiled, but as I smiled and blushed too my mind was in a whirl - London at last, the world of fashion, excitement, Paul. On the other hand, drudgery at the beck and call of two strange French women, one sick, the other old and crotchety, and parting from my parents. Perhaps all our silver clouds have leaden linings, I said to myself.

As Grandmère and I settled for sleep, her snappy old voice whispered in the dark, 'I hope you are pleased with me, my dear. I like a girl of spirit such as I once was myself. I hated to think of such a fine young filly harnessed for life to such a carthorse as that Pierre - though I expect I shall have to take my cane to your back often enough yet. Now, goodnight; you'd better learn at once that I like my eight hours sleep.'

The La Rochelle Bible is in the Heritage Museum.

You can see the weaving loft above the cottages in Turnagain Lane, in the picture in the middle of this book.

TOM COOPER AND THE ARCHBISHOP

'Ah - ah - ah - Tschoo.' The almighty sneeze fluttered the papers from the Headmaster's high desk to the schoolroom floor on a dozy summer afternoon in 1812.

'Sloshed on snuff again,' Tom whispered to his friend Bill Burgess.

'Cooper ! Hold out your hand.' They hadn't heard the usher until his hot garlicky breath hit their necks. Tom quickly held out his left hand for the expected savage cut across the knuckles with the edge of a broken school slate. He had learned to bite his lip to stop the tears, but he couldn't stop the angry red which flooded the left side of his face, where the barely-healed scars of the pellets from Jem's horse-pistol still itched. He had been so lucky to save his sight in that accident last November. If he was ever to be an artist he would need his drawing hand too and was angrily glad he had been quick-witted enough to save it from the usher who now said;

'Chatter and scribble; scribble and chatter - they'll be the death of you, Tom Cooper, have you no duty to work or care for your poor deserted mother ?' Tom was really angry now. How dare that prowler, who terrorised the boys while the Headmaster snoozed, hold his mother up to his schoolmates' scorn?

As they trudged home past the Westgate to the little cottage in its shadow inside the walls of Canterbury, Tom poured out his troubles on to Bill. Father had done a flit when Tom was five, to follow the regiment when it was ordered abroad to fight the French. Mother had stood the gossip and the shame for four long years now, toiling late over her dressmaking to feed and clothe the five young children he had left behind him. With three regiments in town, there were plenty of officers' ladies to order new gowns and poorer local women to pay for altering old ones to keep in fashion. Through one of her customers, his brother William had just got a job pounding pills for Dr Bailey, the Barracks surgeon, so now his path was set for him, like it or not. Lizzie and Sarah had no choice either but to help with the sewing and become needle-slaves in their turn.

'All I can do and all I want to do is to draw, but where's the money in Art ?' Tom sighed.

'I suppose uncle could take you on painting coach-panels if you can't do any better,' said Bill, 'At nine you should be looking round you.'

Tom's heart sank to his hobnail boots. Canterbury meant the tramp of soldiers, the clatter of mail-coaches, the stinks of horses and tanning, the close-packed town in its grey walls. Must he drag out his days endlessly doing the same dreary job? For the first time he felt in his bones why Dad had run away.

Mother greeted him in a fluster. 'Oh, Tom, thank goodness you're home. You can run up to the Precincts, for I promised the Archdeacon's housekeeper that her Sunday black bombazine would be ready today. Remember to go to the side door and if you see any of the quality take your cap off.' Poor Mum, what a life! How could he have envied Dad?, Tom thought as he hurried up the busy High Street and in by the crumbly old gate into the quiet green space round the old Cathedral, just turning pink in the evening light.

His errand done, Tom perched on a bollard and pulled out his slate and chalk for he had nothing else to draw on. The North-West bell tower was the oldest part left above ground. Round, interlaced arches; tic-tac patterns, so different from the soaring arches of the huge central tower or the spread of the west window. His thoughts had taken off, wheeling round the roof-tops like the evening swallows.

'It's a shame all that will turn back into sums tomorrow morning at the flick of a sponge,' a kind voice broke in on him. 'Who taught you to draw so well?' Tom looked up into a round, red face framed in a fine pair of side-whiskers.

'I'm only practising, sir - it's not worth keeping; Mum calls it a waste of time, anyway. I really should be going now, please sir,' said Tom, jumping up.

'Let me at least pay for a most instructive encounter,' said the stranger. 'I must have some pencils about me, for every workman needs his tools, you know.' His many-caped driving coat was stiff with pockets and from each came red, black, blue, long and stumpy pencils. He turned to a quiet, thin boy standing behind him. 'Wake up, George Cattermole - give the lad your drawing-block.' With a smile George handed Tom his very first drawing paper.

'Good luck to you,' he said shyly.

'Good evening to you, young sir,' the strange man broke in. 'If you ever take up an artistic line in life, spare a thought for John Britton,' and, tipping his hat, he handed Tom a trade card and they ran up the steps of a nearby house. Tom was left staring at the elaborate curlicues of the copperplate trade card which bore the legend: 'John Britton; printer- 'the Beauties of Wiltshire;', 'Architectural Beauties of Britain' etc., etc.'

So, some people manage to make a living from drawing or he wouldn't have a young apprentice. I wonder how it is done ? Tom mused as he hurried home.

'Look what I've got !' Tom panted as he burst in. Mother looked up from her sewing.

'Did you deliver my parcel and why were you so long ? I hope you've not been talking to strangers.'

'No, he talked to me,' Tom replied and Mother had to laugh as he told them of his strange meeting.

'I want some of that paper for curl-papers,' Lizzie said.

'Not till I've had some to cut my new bodice pattern,' snapped Sarah.

'You'll only waste more time now, day-dreaming over your sketches,' said William. Only little Annie stuck up for him,

'He can have all the paper and the rest of the pencils if I can borrow the red one to give my doll Jane rosy cheeks - she's poorly from staying indoors every day.'

At bedtime Mother grew serious. 'We've managed to keep our pride and our self-respect so far, but I'll not be beholden to anyone. What we win must be by our own efforts, for you'll soon find out that nothing in this life comes free.' For all that, Tom felt that the Cathedral came free in all its changing moods - every day different, under blue or storm-steely, dawn or evening light. He tried to tuck himself away in odd corners to sketch it in his rare free moments. One day, a white-wigged, black-coated gentleman with a long, thin face stopped to admire Tom's first, full-length view of the Cathedral from the south-west, just as his best soft pencil from Mr Britton broke. Tom looked up at the stranger and said,

'Would you, by any chance, Sir, have a penknife to sharpen this for me, please ?' and hoped that his Mother would think he had been polite enough.

'With pleasure, my boy; I had been reflecting that your sketch there was worth five shillings,' the tall gentleman replied. As he stood, whittling at Tom's pencil with an ivory-handled knife, he kept looking at the drawing and then at the Cathedral with his head first on one side and then on the other.

Portrait of Archbishop Manners Sutton
1755 - 1828

© *Canterbury Museums*

Archbishop Manners Sutton was in office for twenty-three years from when Thomas Sidney Cooper was two years old. By the time they met, the Archbishop was sixty and had eleven children of his own. When as an old man Cooper wrote 'My Life', he said, 'his kind encouragement and generosity to me as a little boy gave me faith in mankind and really acted as the first inducement to persevere in taking up an artistic career.'

'On second thoughts, if you will part with that drawing, boy, I will be glad to give you five pounds for it. You may tell your family that the Archbishop is assured you have a God-given talent for drawing.'

'Please, please, Your Grace, have it as a present! I could not take money for it; Mother would be very vexed with me.' Tom found himself clinging to the august black arm, forgetting altogether how he should talk or behave to an Archbishop of Canterbury.

'No, my son, such a sum may pay for your tuition. It is not fit that we should waste any of God's gifts, even if He also expects us to help ourselves!' He drew out a crackling piece of white paper from his tail-coat pocket. Then one so used to being instantly obeyed swept off serenely, the sketch in his hand, without a backward glance, totally convinced that his command would not fall on deaf ears.

This time Tom did not run but dragged himself home, wondering what to do with this large, stiff white paper which was worth more money than he had ever seen in his short life and which he felt was burning a hole in his pocket. That was what came of talking to strangers, and the Archbishop of Canterbury at that. When at last he came in quietly and dropped the note in Mother's lap and explained how he had come by it, he hardly knew what to expect, but it was certainly not this. She sank to the floor, threw her apron over her head and sobbed as if she would never stop.

'After all we've endured these four years, we'll be ruined and disgraced. Everyone will be sure you stole it ! Who would ever believe such a tale anyway ? - as if His Grace would ever speak to the likes of you. Anyway, I'm sure I don't know what to do with it, for we have never had need of a bank and if it stays here we are sure to be robbed.'

Just then Sarah jumped up to snatch the note and screamed, 'It's not fair - you sit about dreaming and drawing while we work all day; you are scarred and ugly but everyone helps you; you're a boy and can go out and about in the world. What chance have I, with twice your looks, but to wait and hope one day to catch any sort of a husband's eye - if I'm lucky in this dreary old town.'

As she stamped her foot and coloured up, Tom saw his Dad to the life in her and could find her no answer, for he knew he was like her and he knew her words were true. Solid, sensible William came to the rescue, as he always did.

'My Dr Bailey would keep that note safe for you. After all it's worth eight weeks of my wages ! Why don't you let Tom come up to the Barracks with me tomorrow, as it's Saturday ?'

'I just wanted Mother to have the only money I'm likely to win,' said Tom. 'I can't earn like William and the girls. I don't suppose I'll ever have so much again, just from drawing.'

Next day, when William had finished explaining and handed over the money, Dr Bailey scared Tom nearly out of his wits, for he was never still and his words shot out like bullets from his little pursed-up mouth.

'Come here, sit there! Draw that,' he said, pointing to a grey and flabby piece of a human leg in a glass jar full of smelly liquid. 'Hah! You can draw, then. What about painting? What about perspective? You seem to have lost your tongue, boy. Follow me!'

In the little lean-to behind the surgery there was hardly room to stand, what with an easel, a sink, pots of colours, a jar of brushes, some stuffed birds, a case of butterflies and a tall vase of bullrushes.

'My get-away! Everyone needs one, you know. Come on Saturday mornings! No charge! My pleasure! Catch! this is for your Mother. I've changed your bit of paper.'

In the explosive volley of commands Tom just had the wit to catch a paint-stained rag as it flew across the room. In it were tied five shining golden sovereigns.

'Scribble and chatter' did become Tom's fate for nearly ninety more years, until, at the end of his long life, he wrote about his early struggles and about all the people who had helped him on his way, from his school friend Bill Burgess to the Archbishop of Canterbury. As Thomas Sidney Cooper, a rich and famous painter, patronised by Queen Victoria herself, he came back to live in Canterbury. His brother William had been elected Mayor and Tom was able to buy his Mother's old cottage. There he founded and taught in his Art College, which still flourishes today under a new name. He wanted poor people to have the chances he and Sarah never had, so he only charged two old pence a day.

Someone who was later able to use his college was Mary Tourtel, creator of Rupert Bear.

Canterbury Museum ©

Becky worked at the 'Coach and Horses' in the High Street where Louise's father lost his wallet. This drawing is by T S Cooper, the boy in the last story. The Inn stood where the Library and Museum are in the Beaney Institute. Today the County Hotel and the Post Office are on the left hand side of the street.

BECKY, LOUISE AND THE RAILWAY

Seven o'clock of a Tuesday morning in 1828 and two very different days began for two Canterbury girls. Louise woke to angry voices through her bedroom wall. Mother and Father are arguing again, she sighed to herself. I wish railways had never been thought of. Mother's family were millers with their money in a canal scheme, while Father was a banker and could only talk of Mr Stephenson and the plan for a railway to Whitstable. She lay looking up at the pretty muslin drapes above her bed and listened for the horn as the morning 'Tally-Ho' coach swung round the corner by St Dunstan's church to head for London. All her eleven years she had loved to stand at the window of her fine brick home opposite the church and look down the street to the old Westgate. The mail coach from Paris and Dover; the ladies and gentlemen of fashion on the coach from Margate; scarlet-coated officers returning to duty off the London coach; the slow carrier's cart lumbering up St Thomas' Hill towards Whitstable - all had to pass her door. All roads met at Canterbury and the town was full of coaching inns and taverns.

'People can go by coach if they like,' Father would say, 'but we need to get our corn and hops and leather quickly to London by rail and boat.'

'What's wrong with the river?' Mother would snap back, 'The old monks knew it was the way to ship in heavy stone when they built the Cathedral. Father says . . . ,' but that always made Louise's father stamp out slamming the door, for Grandfather Kingsford had never wanted his daughter to marry the young banker he called an unsteady flibbertigibbet.

This morning she found Father in the breakfast parlour looking dreadful. His hair was tousled, his face grey and his pockets were hanging out. He looked up.

'You haven't seen my pocket-book on the stairs, I suppose? I played whist with the officers last night but got involved in a brawl outside the 'Rose and Crown,' where some drunken soldiers were being hauled out. I must have lost it then, but I've only two days to find the money it held or I'll lose my stake in the railway scheme.'

Mother flounced in. 'If you came home at a Christian hour and didn't play for such high stakes we would not have to suffer these ups and downs.' She sat down to her coffee, slitting open her letters savagely with her ivory paper knife.

'Poor Father, I'll look all down the street when I go to my drawing lesson,' Louise whispered.

'Thank you, pet; I'd better get down to the bank quickly,' he answered with a wan smile and, giving a quick peck to his wife's cold cheek, he left.

Meanwhile the seven chimes of the hall clock at the 'Coach and Horses' in the High Street woke Becky that Tuesday morning with a guilty start. She should have been up and about an hour earlier, but it had been well past midnight when the officers and their guest had finished their game and gone home. She had sat yawning in her corner, jerking awake to put more coal on the fire, to replace and trim the guttering candles and fill the wine glasses. She should have cleared up then and there, but she had been on her feet for more than eighteen hours and told herself the morning would do. She knew she was lucky to have a job at all at thirteen, as maid-of-all-work at the busiest inn in town. She had been born in Canterbury workhouse, in the Harlots' Harbour where the unmarried mothers went. When her Mother ran off to London she had been put to a wet nurse, until she was old enough to be taught with the other charity children to scrub, clean and sweep the old stone building by the river, where the old and young, disabled and jobless all ended up when they had no families to help them.

Last night Becky had got really interested in the game. One of the officers was sweating rivulets down the creases of his red, fat face and cursing his bad luck loudly. The other two could have been brothers with their high, aristocratic noses and the high-pitched nasal drawl of their patronising voices, growing ever more edgy as the night wore on. The fourth was a civilian in smart dove-grey clothes, with a rampant crest of light brown hair, a sparkling eye and an intense expression. He had lost heavily at the start of the evening, but his luck had turned and the pile of notes and coin beside him had grown steadily. Only he would thank her with a smile as she did her small tasks round the table; she could have been a ghost for all the notice the others took of her. Rising at last, the taller beak-nosed officer scribbled a note and pushed it across the table.

'That's a draft on my bankers for one hundred pounds - you should let me ride free for life on your precious railway, if it ever gets finished, the way you've stripped me to the bone this evening.'

The civilian pulled out his fob watch. 'Help ! Is it so late ? My wife will make my life a misery if I don't hurry.'

'I'd get the warmest welcome from mine if ever I had such deuced fine luck to bring home,' sighed red-face, ruefully. They crowded to take their greatcoats from the chest by the window and, gathering his scattered wealth, the dove-grey gentleman hurried after them, calling back, 'Thank you, my dear. You remind me of my daughter and should long since have been in your bed.'

'Lucky daughter! I'd like a Dad like that,' Becky thought, 'I wish I could ever find out who my father was - some fly-by-night soldier, I expect.'

In the cold light of morning Becky wrinkled her nose. How she detested the inn's early morning smell of stale wine, stale tobacco smoke and rancid wax. She drew back the curtains, unlatched the shutters and a pale shaft of sunlight showed up the dust, the dirty glasses and the spilt cards. She dropped to her knees with a sigh to gather up the cards and glimpsed a pocket-book half protruding under the antique chest below the bow window. As she picked it up two gold sovereigns fell out, but when she opened it there was only a wad of banknotes and a folded letter she could not read. She quickly stuffed it in her apron pocket as Mrs Jarvis' heavy step sounded outside.

'Lazy little slut! I've half a mind to send you back where you came from - lying abed with last night's mess piled high! Why is the breakfast table not set? You have twenty minutes to catch up on your work or there's no dinner for you today.'

That scolding, nagging voice rang in her ears as she scuttled about. Cook would give me no supper last night after I broke that glass. I can't work day after day without food, Becky thought rebelliously. A bad beginning only got worse. A big party from Dover piled in demanding breakfast. The butter fell off the tray as she forgot that step to the kitchen and she got a cuff on the ear for her clumsiness. The scullery maid was sick so she was set to wash dishes which made her late for polishing the street windows. The porter was giving her the rough edge of his tongue when some ladies tittered past wanting coffee. So it went on to the day's last task - cleaning fifteen pairs of boots, before she flopped exhausted on her straw mattress in the little room behind the pantry. All she had eaten was some left-overs when she was washing up long ago in the morning.

She felt the hard roundness of the two coins pressing through her apron pocket. All that paper's no good, but these coins would get me away, Becky thought, for what is there to stay for ?

I never knew who my father was but my Mother had the sense to run when she could. She knew there were better chances in London for the likes of us.

That was why, on Wednesday morning, as the persistent drizzle fell, a bedraggled little figure with a small bundle paused in the shelter of St Dunstan's porch and stared across the road at the two figures on the doorstep of no.1 London Road.

Louise's Tuesday had been no better than Becky's. When she came home from her sketching lesson, Mother had gone out visiting, so she expected to take luncheon alone, but opening the dining room door she stood rooted to the spot. Father was hunched over the table, his shoulders shaking. He raised a tear-stained face and said,

'We're ruined; how can I tell your Mother ?' Louise ran to kneel beside him. 'Can you tell me about it ? I'll try to understand,' she said, half realising that poor Father just needed somebody to listen and even an ignorant girl would do.

'I borrowed some money from the bank's funds without telling. It was very wrong, but if I couldn't buy railway shares then I would lose my chance to be part of Canterbury's future. I knew I could repay it before anyone noticed, because I have shares in London. Then there was the Stock Exchange collapse last year and I lost that money too. That is why I've annoyed your Mother playing cards, to get the money that way.'

'That's very risky, isn't it?' Louise said. 'I've heard more people lose than win when they gamble.'

'Yes, but Whist isn't just luck, it's skill too and soldiers are not the smartest players. Last night I did really well, but now that is all lost as well and I have a meeting with the bank directors in the morning. I'll have to confess and bankers who lose the trust of customers and partners are finished.'

'Have you checked at the inn?' Louise asked.

'Of course, it was the first place I went, but Mrs Jarvis said they were so busy that lots of people had gone through the room since last night and she had been there herself when the maid was clearing up. We'll have to sell this house - how your grandfather will scoff. Had he been less hard, I'd have tried borrowing from him.'

As they heard Mother returning, Father gave Louise a quick hug. 'Let's say nothing to upset her; I count on my good little actress to keep the rest of the day sweet at all costs.' How hard that had proved, Louise mused, as she lay again in her dainty little bedroom that night.

Now, on Wednesday morning, the low grey sky and drizzle matched their mood as she stood on the steps to see Father off.

'If you do what's right, Father, an old pocket-book of lost money can't matter so very much.' Her voice rang out on the damp air as she added 'Even if we have to sell our house we'll never be as poor as that little girl,' and Louise pointed at Becky.

Becky saw the dove-grey gentleman and knew at once what she had done. Louise saw in that grubby face a reflection of her own; that girl could be the sister she never had. Father was too sunk in gloom to see anything.

With a little shrug Becky started off along London Road, clutching her coins and with every step the battle inside her raged more fiercely. Who had ever tried to help her ? Why should she give up her only chance of freedom? But why did she pity that poor gentleman? And why was she so drawn to that pretty girl on the doorstep? By the time she had gone a hundred paces she had slowed down and after another fifty she stopped and looked back. The man was just turning to wave goodbye. With a deep gulp Becky dropped her bundle and started to run back.

'Stop !' she called out, before she had time to change her mind. The two figures had stopped to stare.

'It is surely my little friend from the 'Coach and Horses,' Father said.

'I think this is yours, sir,' Becky gasped, thrusting the pocketbook at him. 'You dropped it when you got your greatcoat.'

Father stared unbelieving at the wallet, but at Becky with a wry look. 'It's a long time since Monday night ! Where has it been since then and am I right in thinking that it was on its way to London a few minutes ago?'

Louise broke in angrily. 'How can you be so mean and unkind, Father, when she's saved your honour and good name in the nick of time? You are like the man in the fable - if you live in a glass-house you shouldn't throw stones.'

Canterbury Museum ©

Packed in their open carriages and waving flags, everyone is excited on opening day as the train approaches the Whitstable terminus - now Gorell Tank. The harbour had not been built yet so sailing boats were beached at high tide to load with goods for London.

Becky had no idea what they were talking about; she could only think of herself, with her escape thrown away. Clutching at Father's sleeve she implored him, 'Please, please let me stay. You can see I couldn't face Mrs Jarvis, but I could do any rough work and I only had a little wage at the 'Coach and Horses.' Mother appeared on the doorstep.

'Come inside at once, all of you; what a public exhibition! And who is this young person?' She stopped to take a close look at Becky and with a white face clutched the doorpost as if about to faint. With a great effort she spoke, 'How old are you, child, and where do you come from?'

'Thirteen and a half, if you please, and Canterbury Workhouse, Ma'am. My name's Becky.' A sigh very like relief escaped Mother.

Louise turned to her and said, 'You promised me a maid of my own for my twelfth birthday soon. 'I'm sure we could get on, for we even look alike.'

'Yes, dear, I was always sorry you never had sisters or brothers and although once a maid, always a maid, the companionship of a loyal servant is not to be despised.' Mother turned on Father. 'I think no more discussion is needed. I can place this Becky in our household and you had better hurry for the bank directors will not wait all morning.'

'You are right, as you always are, my dear,' said Father with a very serious look. 'I hope to bring back good news this evening,' and he strode off whistling towards the Westgate.

Louise never discovered what skeleton lurked in the cupboard of Mother's family, or was it Father's? She was too happy in a life no longer lonely, with a Becky whose rough edges and sharp temper softened as life treated her better.

On a May morning in 1830, the whole family with Becky in attendance, dressed in their best, hurried to North Lane Station for the grand opening of the railway to Whitstable. They were joining the first people in the world ever to pay to ride even part of the way behind a steam engine. The new Liverpool - Manchester line was behind time and would not open until September.

'It's not often that little Canterbury has a world first,' said Father as he handed them into the 'Adelaide' open carriage, while the band played and the flags waved. Off they glided up the hill, pulled by a cable and down the other side they swooshed at a terrifying 25 miles per hour towards Bogshole. There at last was the 'Invicta' engine waiting, its tall chimney gently belching smoke and its top-hatted driver perched aloft while the fireman shovelled coal into the furnace. With a blast on the whistle 'Invicta' slowly gathered speed for the last miles down to Whitstable harbour.

'There's the sea !' shrieked Louise.

'I've never seen it before,' sighed Becky, happily. The little ships were waiting in the bay to ship Grandfather's grain and flour and Father's customers' hops and leather to London.

'The good times are here again,' said Father, smiling down at Mother.

'I know they are, my dear,' Mother said and held out her hand to him.

George and Robert Stephenson's 'Invicta' locomotive is displayed in the Heritage Museum. It beat the 'Rocket' in carrying passengers by five months. The railway lost money after all and was taken over in 1841 by the company which built Canterbury West Station. Trains ran to and fro to Whitstable until 1952.

HENRIETTA'S FIRE-BOMB

'Hell's bells,' said Henrietta as she slopped Gran's early morning tea. The steep spiral stair which led up from the front room of 10 Broad Street had tripped her up this Friday in the May of 1942. She slurped up the spill in the saucer and knocked. Gran was sitting up as usual, neat and tidy as a doll's house figure, teeth in, hair smooth, shawl round shoulders and Bible open on the turned-down sheet.

'They have set fire upon Thy holy places - Psalm 74,' read Gran. 'I hope that's not a prophecy after what happened to you in Exeter.' Henrietta had been only five weeks with Gran in Canterbury. When Dad joined up and Mum went to work in a government office in London at the beginning of the War, she had gone to boarding school, but Mum had been glad when the school was evacuated to the safety of Devon, before the worst of the London blitz, nearly two years ago. Then, at the end of April this year, Exeter was half-destroyed in a hail of fire-bombs. Behind their brick fronts the old wooden houses had gone up in flames, like bonfire night. Henrietta remembered shuffling to school next morning from her billet through burnt paper, piled up in the spring streets like autumn leaves, until her legs and socks were black to the knees. Mum had come down the next day to bring her back to live with Gran. She only had a short walk now to the girls' school in the old hospital building. She looked at her watch - Help! half an hour for dressing, breakfast and that last bit of Maths homework.

'Don't bother with my breakfast, I'll be down soon,' Gran called. 'I've got to go to the food office about your ration book. It's no good hoping for fish although it's Friday, but it might be worth queuing for sausages and cat-scraps for Sukey.' Henrietta thought, 'Blow that fat, black, self-satisfied lump of a cat. Sukey's fed better than Gran herself.' Sukey had ruled the household before Henrietta arrived and kept up a cautious hostility, as she glared balefully with her yellow eyes from the safety of Gran's knee.

As she rushed round her attic room packing her satchel and glad it was nearly the week-end, Henrietta stopped to brush her hair by her little dormer window and look at the best view of the Cathedral in all Canterbury. Beyond the city wall with its curved bastion opposite, Bell

Harry Tower soared this fine May morning, the smaller towers of so many dates clustered round its base like so many little birds, their beaks upward. She turned away with a shiver, remembering how Exeter Cathedral had survived the fire-storm of the big raid although the choir school had been hit and a boy killed.

Nobody concentrated at school that day; was it the lovely summer weather or the sick suspense? Was it Canterbury's turn next? When she reached home that evening Gran was snappy after a trying day of forms and queues and shortages. It was vegetable stew again, with an Oxo cube, for there had been no sausages left at the butcher's.

The week-end seemed to drag by; Saturday was baking hot and Sundays were always boring after church; Gran was old-fashioned and believed in a day of rest without cooking. Even she was restless and out of sorts by evening.

'It's been far too hot for May; I'll be glad to see the first of June.
I'm off to bed after the 9 o'clock news and I'll hope to wake in a better mood,' she said. The news was full of the RAF's 900-bomber raid on Cologne.

'They've got a cathedral too, haven't they?' Henrietta asked.

'Yes,' said Gran. 'My friend Mabel once brought me a bottle of Eau-de-Cologne after a Rhine cruise, the bag had a picture of a big church on it. Your grandfather would never take me there - he said he'd had enough of abroad, fighting in the trenches in the first World War. You couldn't talk to the men who came back alive, too many of their mates had died and none of us at home knew what it was really like - all that mud, stink and suffering.'

Henrietta saw that Gran did not want old memories raked up but still went up to bed saying 'WASTE - waste for everyone on both sides in this endless war,' which had gone on since she was eight. She had to screw up her eyes hard to remember that last pre-war summer on the sands at Broadstairs and Dad running after the bolting donkey to which she clung, splashing through the pools with his trousers rolled up to the knee. When she had blown out her candle she pulled back the black-out curtain to take a last look at Bell Harry, serene in the summer dusk.

She woke from a dream where she was helping Grandpa with his bees and a swarm had attacked them. The drone was deafening as she sat upright and realised it was the siren's wail that had wakened her and the hum of many aircraft. She rushed to the window. The whole city was lit up by brilliant chandeliers. Blue and yellow flares were hanging in the sky and blood-red ones were drifting from the Cathedral towards their end of town. She looked at her watch - 12.45 - just the time the Exeter raid had begun. She collided at the foot of the stairs with Gran.

'I was just coming up for you, we must get to the cupboard by the chimney stack - but where's Sukey ?' They always went to that cupboard when the siren went. Gran's neighbour at number 9 was a builder and had told them that, as the cottages were built round the chimney, even if the building collapsed the stack would give them a lee to shelter under until they were dug out. There wasn't much room in the cupboard with Sukey's laundry basket taking up most of the floor space.

'I'll see if she's sheltering in the privy,' Henrietta called, dashing out of the kitchen door. The 'little house' with its earth toilet was at the end of the backyard, but no Sukey was there. As she turned back to the cottage she thought she heard a mew from the roof.

'Drat that cat, she must take her chance; at least we'll have more room to shelter,' Henrietta muttered rebelliously as she hurried back. 'She's not there. Can I put the basket out to make more room for our Thermos and biscuits?' Henrietta reported. Gran sighed and said,

'Tip it on its side; she's sure to come soon; she's had enough practice lately with all those sirens.'

'She minds more about that cat than me,' Henrietta thought, but just then the crump of a big bomb and a string of lesser thumps set up a shaking round them and set them shaking too. Henrietta's teeth were chattering although it was getting very hot in the cupboard. As they sat holding trembling hands, she could sense that Gran was reciting prayers to herself non-stop. Then she saw a tear course down Gran's left cheek and her heart melted.

'Let me see if Sukey's under your bed, too frightened to come out,' she said and before Gran could stop her she was off up the spiral stair. She stopped, appalled, in Gran's room. She too must have pulled back the

Paul Crampton © The new Courthouse is just to the right of this picture with No. 10 beyond that, but you can see how near the bombs and fires spread towards Henrietta. This photograph of Lady Wootton's Green shows the clearing up beginning. Today you will see a row of new houses. The Great Gate and buildings of St Augustine's Abbey at the rear were scarred but left standing. They are now part of the King's School.

blackout for, through the window, the whole city seemed ablaze. The smoke and flames rose so high she could not see the Cathedral but inside the walls, as far as the eye could see, the whole top end of the town nearest to her was on fire. There was no sign of Sukey and, guiltily remembering that mew, she realised that the dormer in the back room led on to the roof beside the chimney stack.

A bucket of sand and a bucket of water stood each side of the chair by the window, so Henrietta jumped up, pushed open the casement and climbed out. To her left she felt waves of heat and could hear crackling. A string of fire-bombs must have landed in Lady Wootton's Green beside the Abbey gate and she saw with horror flames licking along the cottage roofs next to theirs and, yes, there was Sukey mewing pitifully. As she looked she saw a smouldering fire-bomb was lodged in the angle between their roof and the next. She knew you must first smother it with sand but that bucket was too heavy to heave through the window.

'I'll fill a pillow-case first,' she thought as she scrambled back,' then I should be able to carry the half-empty bucket.' Tucking her nightie into her school knickers, she shoved the full pillow-case up to the window-sill and herself after it. The first few puny handfulls of sand she chucked made no difference to the smouldering bomb, so she swung the pillow-case hoping it would land on the bomb. Only half of it did and as she smelt the cotton case charring she knew she must hurry. Lying on her tummy across the sill she just managed to heave up the half-empty bucket and edged on her bottom across the tiles. 'I daren't stand up here. I'll just have to throw the bucket too,' she said to herself. It landed with a thump behind the little cylinder bomb which began to roll, but oh so slowly, towards the edge of the roof to hang for a moment before falling to land in the yard, where it could burn itself out harmlessly. The bucket had rolled too but its rim had caught on a gutter fixing and, by gingerly putting out her left foot, Henrietta was able to hook it towards her by its handle. Now for Sukey. If she concentrated fiercely on one thing at a time she might stop her chattering teeth from shaking her whole body to bits. Mesmerised by the flames on the far roof, Sukey was deaf to the calls of her old enemy.

'She hates water even more than me.' Henrietta reflected. 'I'll throw some just behind her to drive her this way.' Once more she scrambled back to tip just enough water into the sand bucket to drag up with her again. Slurp, splash ! A satisfactory slop of water landed with a thud on the roof slope behind Sukey and, with an indignant yowl, a big, black, wet bullet shot past Henrietta and through the open window to bolt down the stairs.

'I'd better dowse what I can of our roof with the rest of the water,' Henrietta thought to herself, but that last effort seemed to drain her empty too. She and Gran clung together, wet, dirty and frightened at the foot of the stairs as the crackling sound from next door came ever closer. A thump on the front door startled them.

'Anyone there ? Come on out before the hoses start.' They opened up to two black-faced firemen. 'The warden here will take you up to the old hospital, but we must get this blaze under before this end of Broad Street goes the way of St George's parish. We're the only ones to spare, for we've only just arrived from Ashford.'

Sukey was put protesting into the fish basket, the Air Raid Warden fetched a blanket for Gran and Henrietta grabbed her winter coat from its hook. Back they went to the building she had only left after school on Friday, to find the hallway full of folk like themselves, bombed out from cottages opposite. As they sat down everyone sighed with relief at the sound of the 'All clear:' the time was 2.10am in the early morning of June 1st. Henrietta felt she would never unwind, never sleep again, as those terrifying moments on the roof re-ran through her head like an old film. She must have dropped off for the next she knew was the familiar figure of her headmistress, unusually dressed in pyjamas and raincoat. As she gave them tea and sandwiches Miss Blackith said, 'I was bombed out too, you know.'

Later that Monday they were allowed back to 10 Broad Street. As they picked their way over the snaking fire hoses in the street they could hardly take in that their whole familiar landscape had vanished, as if a giant child had snatched up his bricks and thrown them everywhere. From the top of the High Street only the burnt out shell of St George's church and its tower stood among the ruins. Down Burgate a gap had opened up on the right revealing the length of the Cathedral, ringed by the spent fire-bombs, thrown from the roof by the fire-watchers. They reached their front door to find that the fire had stopped near their left-hand wall. Over the ugly gap full of rubble beside them they could see across the ruined buildings the chipped but standing towers of the Abbey gate. They couldn't face the clearing up but, before she went to bed, Henrietta said good night to Bell Harry Tower, still standing like a miracle.

———————◯———————

On a June afternoon in 1997 a tourist coach halted illegally beside the Broad Street car park to let out two people. The comfortable elderly figure, in the sensible shoes and unfashionable cotton dress paused for a moment at Lady Wootton's Green. The impatient, dancing girl at her side said, 'I can't wait, Grandma Hetty, I'm dying for the toilet.' They hurried past the forbidding brick frontage of the new Court House and, with a start, Grandma stopped at a door numbered 10.

'It didn't have an indoor toilet then but maybe it has now. I lived here in the war, you know,' she said, pressing the bell.

'Can I help you, Madam,' a young man answered in a pale and willowy voice, 'This is a lawyer's office; have you an appointment?'

'I never thought to see this cottage standing; it so nearly burned down when I lived here during the Canterbury blitz,' he heard her reply. 'Might my grand-daughter borrow your toilet?'

'In that case, Madam, I might be able to make an exception; please follow me.'

Henrietta stepped over the familiar sill into a strangely spruce interior - but there was the spiral staircase and there was the chimney breast, but where was the cupboard?

'The restorers put in a passage one side and a toilet the other by taking out the cupboards round the chimneystack ,' the young man said, 'but they did retain one interesting old feature - if you look up there you'll see some charred beams dating from the wartime.'

Henrietta realised she could never make this young man see that terrible night of fifty-five years ago with her eyes. Those beams revived too many of her own memories and her sense of loss, when Gran died so soon after, in her sleep, tidy as a doll's house figure in her bed. She had gone back to London and the rest of her life.

'Could I just show my grand-daughter the view from my old bedroom window?' she asked.

'I shall have to accompany you, for security, of course,' said pale-face. There was the dormer window, there the age-old city wall and there stood Bell Harry.

'We really suffer from the tourists these days - sometimes there are 150 coaches a day - in and out in a couple of hours. It must have been much quieter in your day,' came the condescending voice.

'**Now** can we go to McDonalds?' said an insistent small voice beside her.

'If only you both knew,' Henrietta sighed to herself.

Today's Barton Court Grammar School began as the Girl's Technical School in the old Hospital in Longport, where the St Augustine's Abbey Visitors' Centre now stands. I discovered Miss Blackith's role on 1st June 1942 when I later taught at Barton Court. My own experiences as an evacuee in the Exeter blitz come into the story too.